MY NEIGHBOR
MR. LERNER

MY NEIGHBOR MR. LERNER

Martín Anderson

MY NEIGHBOR MR. LERNER

iUniverse books may be ordered through booksellers or by contacting:

iUniverse
1663 Liberty Drive
Bloomington, IN 47403
www.iuniverse.com
844-349-9409

Because of the dynamic nature of the Internet, any web addresses or links
contained in this book may have changed since publication and may
no longer be valid. The views expressed in this work are solely those
of the author and do not necessarily reflect the views of the publisher,
and the publisher hereby disclaims any responsibility for them.

Any people depicted in stock imagery provided by Getty Images are
models, and such images are being used for illustrative purposes only.
Certain stock imagery © Getty Images.

ISBN: 978-1-6632-3128-4 (sc)
ISBN: 978-1-6632-3129-1 (e)

Library of Congress Control Number: 2021922206

Print information available on the last page.

iUniverse rev. date: 07/21/2022

DEDICATION

This work is dedicated to my dear mother Lydia who sacrificed so much to instill the love of learning, and education in her three sons.

Bendición mami. Te quiero mucho.

Little did I know that after meeting our neighbor Mr. Lerner my life would never be the same. In actuality hopelessness and the sensation of running in place and not going anywhere started way before we got to know each other. Yet who he was and what he did, both good and evil, served as the catalyst for events that made me realize that there will be moments in life when being safely involved from a distance, will simply not be enough. What I ultimately learned from that period of my life is that for some of us, there is no hiding place. There is no time for crying with arms outstretched to the heavens asking, "Why me, God, why me?" For better or worse there are those who have a calling with destiny. And we are protected from harm, even death so that we can make the choice to ultimately meet our fate head on or to run away. If we are strong enough we will say, "Yes I am ready!" Or we can choose to escape into frivolous thoughts, to hide, to ignore and even justify a meaningless existence with self - serving gestures about peace, love, and tranquility. But God, by whatever name you want to call her or him, has no interest in your good deeds if anyone and I do mean anyone, on this earth is crying and suffering afflictions caused by those who seek nothing but power and domination.

My story begins with me looking out of my window on an ordinary day.

CHAPTER 1

This is such a beautiful day. I love the feel of the heat and the bright sunshine coming through our living room windows, especially after the cold and nasty below - zero weather that we had this winter. Snow can be lovely when it first falls, but then it starts getting soiled by the dirt and grime that our fair city can produce. But today, the birds are singing their sweet sounds and the kids are out playing catch in the street and basketball at the playground. The other day the older kids on the block even opened the fire hydrant down the street. I gladly trade the joyful expressions on the children's faces for the inconvenience of showering with reduced water pressure. Although not all of my neighbors felt the same way and the firemen came quickly to turn it off as soon as they received a phone call from people who were irate over not having enough water to make suds with their shampoo.

There is Mr. Lerner, standing in front of his building. Even in this heat his pants are neatly ironed with a sharp crease and his long sleeves are slightly rolled up, allowing just enough heat to escape and keep him cool. I don't believe that I have ever seen Mr. Lerner in an argument with anybody, let alone raise his voice. He is always calm, cool, and collected. His tenants say that he's really kind, and when Joaquin Lopez got laid off, and was having trouble making the rent, Mr. Lerner did not even ask for his money. He gave Joaquin time to get back on his feet and find another job. Joaquin along with his wife and three children did not have to find another place to live, thanks to Mr. Lerner's patience and understanding.

"Oh. I didn't even hear you come in the door." I say, as I am a bit startled to see my lovely wife standing behind me. The loudness of my thoughts didn't let me hear Amber opening the door and walking into our home. Getting lost in my mind with competing thoughts is a frequent occurrence for me these days.

"Speaking of that honey. When am I going to feel you come into my garden of love?"

It takes me a second to catch her drift.

"Has it been that long?" It wasn't a good thing that I even had to ask the question.

I feel her velvety soft skin as she gently takes a hold of my face and pulls it away from the window so that I am facing her. Then she whispers,"By our standards, yes it has been. Don't worry about it honey, I'll help you get back on track tonight." She ends this little exchange about our love life with a kiss.

"Dinner smells delicious Josh. Aren't you the chef with the mashed potatoes and fried chicken?!"

"'Do you notice how he's always drinking coffee? How old do you think he is babe?"

"I don't know Josh. Who?"

"Mr. Lerner."

"He has to be at least 70." Amber is more interested in pouring herself a glass of cold water from the kitchen sink than my curiosity over our neighbor.

"Whatever age he is, he's in damn good shape. He goes out there every winter shovels the sidewalk in front of his building even when we get that thick snow and it's extremely cold. When spring comes he starts carefully working on the perennials and shrubs in the community garden. And he sweeps the stairs everyday while barely resting. I feel sorry for him. He seems lonely like he's always lost in his head."

"Why the sympathy Josh? He's white, obviously has a little bit of money saved up and is in good health."

"You gotta be kidding me right?"

"Only halfway honey."

"Anyway, It's almost time to eat. Did you see Danny outside?"

"Yeah, I let him go on playing stickball with his friends. He was having so much fun and you know how they can't wait for summer."

"Me and them both. By the way, how did things go today for the world's greatest public defender?" In the courtroom Amber was a fierce lioness defending her cubs. She took on crooked cops, racist judges, the whole system that preyed on unsuspecting kids trying to gain power in a world that was hell bent on them not having it.

"Oh the usual, I had five thousand clients brought in

by our city's finest. And by some coincidence they were all Black or Puerto Rican can you believe it? Josh.. Hello earth to Josh."

I keep staring at Mr. Lerner, as Amber's voice moved into the background. I see him take a sip of his coffee, and with one smooth motion wave a pesky fly away. Then he looks up at me in my living room window and smiles hello.

"What? I'm sorry honey I was saying hello to Mr. Lerner. He just looked up and noticed me."

"Josh you're going to make him uncomfortable."

"I sincerely doubt it. That guy looks like absolutely nothing can rattle him. Well let's get ready to eat. I'm going to call Danny. "Danny............. come on up, time to eat."

"Do I have to? The game's not over pop."

"Yes. You ask the same question every night."

"All right! See you tomorrow guys. Don't forget we're winning five to four!"

Danny comes up and washes his hands while Amber and I continue setting the table. By the chocolate ice cream stains, I can tell that he hasn't washed his Yankees t-shirt in a few days.

"Bendición pop. Hi mom."

"So your Dad get's a blessing and I just get a hi?"

"No....., yemma, get's a big hug!"

"I'll take that any day! …. Josh, by the way, don't forget that we have dinner coming up with your dad soon."

"You sure look out for the old man don't you?"

"He will always have a special place in my heart. He

stood up for me when your mother admonished you for marrying an Algerian woman. Which seemed really strange considering that she didn't marry a Jewish man."

"We both know the difference is that pop isn't an Arab. And if I may make a correction, I married a beautiful Algerian woman."

"Thank you....... honey"

We share a kiss and the tenderness of her lips, even if just for that brief second, make me truly want to close the distance that she talked about earlier.

"Pop, how come we don't pray before we eat?"

"I don't know. We just never built it in to our routine I guess."

"They always pray before they eat at Jimmy's house."

"That's because they're Pentecostal."

"So what are we?"

"We are kind loving people. But you know that I couldn't wear this pant suit if I was a member of their church." Amber added.

"Can't wear pants? That's not fair!" Said Danny"

"That's right it isn't fair, but that's how it is when it comes to religion. Some things about it are beautiful and others are just plain wrong. Now let's eat."

Danny looks at me, taking in and thinking about what I said, then he comes back to more important thoughts for a kid.

"Can I play with my baseball cards later?"

"Yes, but not too late. You have to get up early for day camp tomorrow."

"I don't want to go tomorrow, it's library day."

"Great! You'll be able to get some good books to read for the summer."

"I can't wait..." Said Danny with a hint of sarcasm.

"Well at least dinner was delicious."

He is coming around but reading isn't necessarily his favorite thing to do.

"And still the mashed potatoes and fried chicken champion of the world...... Josh Blume!"

I hold my arms up like a boxer who has just been declared the winner of a grueling fifteen rounds match.

"Take it easy there, champ. You might want to save some of that energy for later."

I love it when Amber winks at me like that. It only means one thing. Work and anything else will cease to exist and we will get to that special place together.

"Danny help us with the dishes." Says Amber.

"But a....we just finished."

"You do want to play with your baseball cards before going to bed don't you?"

"Yeah mom."

When everything is done and Danny is in his room sleeping, Amber and I were so ready for our time alone.

"Come here. I need you to kiss me gently tonight. Then I will put my arms around you as if you are the only person in the world." Amber tells me as she delivers on her promise of passion.

"Well......, I don't understand. What do you mean?"

"Mr. Blume, How can I clear things up for you?"

"I think I get it, How about if I put my two lips softly on the side of your neck? Right here, on the spot where I gently lift your beautiful black hair. Yesss. This is where I will place my first kiss."

"Your initial kiss is so well placed Mr. Blume...... Ummmm"

I become so excited that I push her against the dresser, and we almost knock over our most recent family picture. Then I take off my shirt and t-shirt all in one motion. She takes off her beautiful silk blouse and we create a pile of clothes that is no longer necessary. She slowly lowers the zipper on her skirt, but lets me do the rest.

"I know how much you love to do that honey."

As I take off her skirt she does that ever so slight wiggle and the skirt slides off her beautiful hips and down her shapely legs. She puts her arms around my neck and pulls me down on top of her.

"Now remember what I said honey. I want you right here with me."

"Amber, Amber this is exactly where I want to be."

At that moment words are no longer needed and time is suspended for both of us. We had entered the sweet sanctuary that was our lovemaking. The doubt of the futility of my work was gone. Afterwards we both came up for air. It was as if our minds could only take so much bliss.

"Honey don't you get tired of the endless line of defendants. Kids who could have been genius inventors, engineers or whatever are converted into petty criminals by this factory of mass production for evil and there is no end in sight."

Amber looks at me and is a bit annoyed that I would bring this up at this moment. And she is right. "Have a lot on your mind don't you? This is nothing new. What makes things so different now? It's what we signed up for."

"I know it is, but for once I need to stop running in circles like a dog chasing its tail." I am laying on the bed, staring up at the ceiling.

"That's the price we pay for being optimistic fools. I look for small victories wherever I can find them. Understand. I refuse, to lose. This world will be a better place for Danny and his children, when his time comes. You do believe that don't you Josh?"

"I did. Not quite sure if that's still the case. Something is slowly eating away at me and I don't know what. I need to figure this out. The other day, I was on my way to seeing a kid who got arrested for stabbing his best friend. He was teaching him a lesson for playing bad defense and losing a pick up basketball game. These feelings came over me and I pulled the car over and started to cry almost uncontrollably."

Amber looked at me a bit perplexed. "You had to pull over? Why didn't you tell me?"

I cover my face with my hands and rubbed my forehead. "I don't know why. Lately every time I see a man with holes in his clothes and dirty begging for change, a woman so addicted to heroin that she sells her body to make enough money for her and her husband to get high, a twelve year old kid willing to obey orders to kill, the first thought that comes to mind is that they all started off as babies, innocent babies.

Amber takes a deep breath and looks at me as if she can't believe how naive I am sounding. "Josh honey, you know that babies are not born under innocent circumstances. This is a messed up world. Some are born with silver spoons in their mouths and all the advantages in the world. While others well, you know what I mean. The problem is, why is this all hitting you so hard now? Whatever it is you know that I'm right here with you right?" She takes my hands from my face and places them next to her heart. Then she holds me and for that moment any doubt about my work is gone. I feel at peace. She strokes my hair and my soul is at ease, if only for the rest of the night. We fall asleep curled up in each other's arms. The next morning I wake up angry and confused. I overslept but I don't think that I even cared.

CHAPTER 2

"I'm late! I can't believe that I didn't hear the alarm clock! Damn it! I have to meet a new 17 year old kid at the detention center today. Amber...! Amber!"

"No need to scream. I'm right here in the living room!"

I put on the first pair of jeans and shirt that I can find, put on my shoes and get ready to leave. "I'm sorry babe. I have to run. Please make sure that Danny takes his inhaler with him today."

"Yes sir! Well don't look at me like that with your arms crossed. If you don't like being talked to like you're a drill sergeant, don't give me orders. I know his schedule and I know what he needs."

"You're right. I'm sorry. I'm just late and in a hurry."

"Look at you, you have on two different kinds of shoes." She looks down at my feet in disbelief.

"Man. I'm really thinking about this kid I'll be seeing today. My caseload is already at one million."

"So one more won't make a difference. Go, go, go" Amber motions with her arms and hands helping me move faster.

As I am leaving our place I see Mr. Lerner. He is getting ready to paint the front door of his building. Look at that John Spencer has another parking ticket on his car. The warmth of the bright sun on my skin feels so good and for a brief second takes my mind away from work. This weather makes battling traffic on the expressway much easier.

All right just two exits to go and I'm there on time! What the hell is going on? No, no, no. My exit is blocked! I can smell something burning. There it is a furniture delivery van on fire on the shoulder of road. And of course everybody has to slow down and see what's happening. Damn it! Now I'm going to be late.

It's not too bad, I'm only ten minutes late but Detective Schmidt is still going to be his usual sweet self. I go through the metal detector and show my ID to the guard, and I walk through the corridor lined with guards, detectives and social workers sitting and working at their desks, on their never ending supply of cases.

"Hey Blume. You're right on time as usual."

"I'm sorry. Traffic was all messed up."

"Don't worry about it. I have your latest "project" ready to meet you."

"And I'm sure you can't wait to give me all the details."

Schmidt seems to relish in other people's misery. It's almost as if he gets happier with every kid that is locked up.

"Look this son of a bitch is lucky that he's 5 months away from his eighteenth birthday. If you ask me for my opinion he should be tried and locked up as an adult. He deserves to be booty bait in the big house."

"Why?" I ask.

"For starters, last week this punk slapped his foster mother around. He's a wizard of wall street, regular young entrepreneur that got arrested for the first time at age twelve for selling pot and carrying a pistol in school. All scholars need protection you know. Do you want me to go on or do you want to talk to him about how he is a 'victim' of society and his surroundings?" Schmidt says this while pretending to play the violin.

This cold hearted fool would never understand even if I took five hours to explain. I mean look at him standing there grinning with his Marine buzz cut and his black wrinkled suit. It seems like he doesn't have an empathetic bone in his body.

"No Detective Schmidt. I'll get all of the information I need from him."

"Great. I'll call and have the guards bring over Mr. Future of Black America right now."

A guard answers the phone. "D - Wing here."

"Yeah. This is Schmidt. Bring me Benson. Samuel Benson. His savior, I mean, his Social Worker, Mr. Blume would like to see him."

"Lovely Schmidt. You don't miss an opportunity to take a shot in here or on the street do you?" Ordinarily I would have kept that comment to myself, but Schmidt has a knack for bringing out what would ultimately be the best in me.

"I don't know what you mean. Better yet mind your business, Blume. You shouldn't be talking about things you don't know. It could be bad for your health. Besides, isn't that what you want to do anyway, save him? I want to see your face about a week from now. This case is going to surprise even you. It doesn't fit the usual profile. This kid has his own way of making his way in the world." I start to see traces of anger in Schmidt's face when he talks about Samuel.

"I like him already, seems like he kind of gets under your skin Schmidt. I'll be waiting in my office."

Why would I even pay attention to Schmidt? He has found at least three dead suspects at crime scenes with 'Saturday Night Specials' on their body. And according to the reports the shooter was nowhere to be found, no witnesses or leads.

I need to get these pile of papers on my desk in order today. Where is his file? Benson, Benson. Yes. Here it is. Parents died when he was ten, then he was taken to live with his grandparents. They decided that they were too old to care for him. He has flunked twice and didn't finish High School. Yet all of his test scores rank him as highly intelligent. He is more than likely your typical kid who becomes bored with school because he isn't being challenged and has figured out that the history that is being taught is full of vicious lies meant to domesticate.

"Blume. ..... Blume!"

"Oh, I'm sorry, Schmidt. I didn't hear you knocking."

"Samuel Benson meet Mr. Blume. He will be your Social Worker."

"Come on in Samuel. It's nice to meet you. Okay you don't have to shake my hand."

"Don't tell me what I already know." Samuel says without hesitation and it takes me only seconds to feel his self confidence. He is definitely not putting on an act.

"What's the matter Blume. You look a little confused?"

"Thank you Schmidt. I'll take it from here. Can I please have some time with Samuel?"

"You sure can. For the next few months you'll have all the time you want with him. Isn't that right Sammy my boy?"

I ignore Schmidt as he walks away and I turn to Samuel. "Please sit down. Tell me about yourself. Do you like basketball?"

"What kind of stereotypical bullshit is that? Yeah I play ball and I love chicken and watermelon too!"

"I asked because you're tall and muscular not because you're Black." I can tell that he isn't offended. Control of the conversation is what he wants.

"I'm just messing with you Mr. Blume. Relax. Look I'm really not in the mood for talking today."

"I understand. I guess we can talk tomorrow. I'll call D-Wing and ask them to come for you."

"Can I wait out there?"

"Sure. Schmidt referred to you as some type of financial genius."

"Probably because I'm not like those fools on the street.

Having fancy cars and clothes don't mean a thing if your ass is flat broke. People who are looking to make money, know with me, that they can talk business. Are you looking to invest?"

He says this without hesitation or concern that I would alert the law about his offer. And with the same poise and confidence, he points to a chair outside of my office, letting me know that he is going to sit down.

Schmidt surprises me a few minutes after Samuel walks out of my door.

"Back so soon Schmidt? Did you forget something?"

He walks into my office without knocking and sits down.

"Make yourself right at home."

"So did you convince the kid that the world is the problem and not him?"

"What are you talking about Schmidt?"

"Benson. Samuel Benson. How did it go, and why is he sitting out there?"

I can't remember the last time that Schmidt asked me about my work with a kid.

"Good to see that you care about him." I say.

"I'm concerned about the youth of America. Don't you know that by now Blume?"

"Samuel wasn't in the mood for talking. I'll catch up with him later."

Schmidt looks at me and smiles in the way that a school yard bully does before getting ready to punch you. He gets up from the chair and buttons up his blazer.

15

"You just let me know if you have any problems with our friend Samuel."

"I'll be just fine. Thanks anyway."

He leaves and says that he is taking Samuel back to the D- Wing.

I call out to him; "Hey Schmidt, I can call the guards to take him back."

"Don't worry Blume, I got it."

This gives me a chance to call his foster mother and learn a little bit more about his situation. Now where is his file? I just had it here before he came in with Schmidt. Alright, here it is! Her name is Mrs. Dolores Bridges. She is one of the best in the system. Let me give her a call and see what is going on with Sam.

CHAPTER 3

"Hello." She answers after three rings.

"Hello. Mrs. Bridges?"

"Yes this is Mrs. Bridges. How can I help you?"

"How have you been? It's Joshua Blume from the Jackson Juvenile Detention Center."

"Blume, Blume..... I remember you. You're that nice Jewish boy aren't you?"

"I guess you could say that." I find no need to bore her with my thoughts on what it means to live life as a Secular Jew. "Thank you for remembering me Mrs. Bridges. I was wondering if we could set up a time to talk about Samuel Benson. You can come here or I would be more than happy to come visit you."

"It's so sad how that boy has turned out. You would have to come here Mr. Blume. You know that I have so much work to do, besides I would have to take two buses to get there."

"No problem at all Mrs. Bridges. Is it okay with you if I come at 11?"

"Eleven, eleven, well let me think. I have to wash the

children's clothes and make sure that I have everything ready for dinner. I should be able to fit you in but it won't take too much time will it Mr. Blume? I mean it's sad and all but I really don't have too much to say about that boy. Lord knows that I don't ever give up on these kids but I no longer have the patience of Job when it comes to that boy. God as my witness I tried."

"That's really unfortunate Mrs. Bridges. Don't worry I won't take up too much of your time."

"I know you won't Mr. Blume. I have God's work to do. Good bye."

Let me start working on this report. It shouldn't take me too long and I have an hour before I head out to see Mrs. Bridges. My sense of time has always been abysmal and as very often happens, I lose track of it and started rushing out of the office at 10:45. I run right past Maria.

"Josh Blume, didn't your mother teach you any manners?"

"No need. She knew that you would Maria."

"Where are you headed?"

"I'm on my way to Mrs. Bridges'."

"Woo! Be careful. It can get a little hot over there."

"Don't worry about me. I'm a big boy, but thanks anyway." I pretend to flex muscles that I don't even have, before leaving the office and getting in my car. It doesn't take me long to get close to the neighborhood.

Driving down this street is depressing. There they are, the local addicts, ready to start their day of waxing poetic on the current state of global affairs but first they need to inject that magic poison that will pollute the rivers of their veins with an intoxicating joy. That guy throwing his arms high in the air and making big circles like a tornado while frenetically dancing on the edge of his life and the sidewalk, is completely gone! He almost gets run over by a van going about forty miles an hour, and doesn't even notice. The lines, wrinkles and scars on his battle worn face do not match his completely black hair. Those five guys in front of that abandoned building look organized and ready to kill anyone who gets in the way of their business. They won't hesitate to shoot any rival that is foolish enough to try to sell dope in their territory. I see a kid at the corner who must only be about ten years old. He serves as their perfect underage look out for the cops. He has a subtle strut and is all decked out in his designer blue jeans, a black shirt and immaculately white polished gym shoes.

I call out to him. "Hey kid."

"What you need is down there man." He points to a building about half way down the street.

"I don't need anything. What are you doing out here?"

"Fuck you! Don't worry about what I'm doin. Why is you wastin my time talkin man!"

He turns around, looks at the guys near the building and lifts his arm.

"All right. No need to call your boys. I'm just asking that's all. I was concerned about you. Looks like your paper route is really working for you."

"What!? Is you deaf man? I said don't worry about me! Worry about your damn self!"

As I get closer to Mrs. Bridges' home all of a sudden her block looks like it doesn't even belong in this part of town. It is an oasis in the middle of the craziness, chaos and violence. The red bricked church on the corner has a sign on the bottom that reads 1871. Every single lawn looks freshly cut. The Block Club sign proudly invites new members to meetings that are held the first Tuesday of every month. There is not a piece of garbage or dog poop to be found on the sidewalk or in the grass. There are no broken windows in any of the homes. I park on the street and make my way to her door, and ring the bell.

She opens the door and there is a sweet and delightful smell coming from the oven.

"Come on in Mr. Blume." She finishes drying her hands on her apron, smiles warmly and steps to the side welcoming me in to her home.

"Oh my goodness Mrs. Bridges, I'm right on time, aren't I? It smells like heaven."

"I thought you wanted to talk about Samuel Benson. You're going to make me think that you came over just for my peach cobbler son. Ha, ha."

Mrs. Bridges has a hearty laugh that can warm the coldest heart. And she didn't turn down the volume. She is a proud Black woman definitely comfortable in her own skin.

"Mrs. Bridges. You're looking quite well these days."

"If quite well is another word for fat. Well then thank you."

"You know I didn't mean it that way."

"I know son. I'm just playing with you. I know how sensitive you can be. You come down to this neighborhood in that white long sleeve shirt with your plaid tie and blue jeans. You know you stick it out like a sore thumb, don't you? Not so much on this block but when you go down the street, you're likely to get arrested by the police who will probably mistake you for a customer. Most white people don't come here for nothing else no way."

"Yes. I know you're right. Don't you ever feel afraid living here."

"Of what? He was and is a fisher of men. So I am here, the Lord's will be done."

"Maybe some day we can talk about why that work never ends, Mrs. Bridges."

"We will. Please sit Mr. Blume. Would you like some lemonade or water?"

"Water would be nice. Thank you. I don't remember that painting of the last supper being there the last time I was here. Is it new?"

"Not that new son. See, Jesus is talking to the treacherous one who is going to betray him for thirty pieces of silver." She points at Judas. So that I know exactly who she is talking about.

"Well maybe he thought that Jesus had already betrayed him and his people. He had promised to deliver them from the cruelty of the Roman Empire. Then he tells the twelve that he is going to voluntarily surrenderer without even a fight? Wouldn't you feel betrayed Mrs. Bridges?"

"I don't even think about all that foolishness son. There's power in the blood! All I know is that my Jesus is here whenever I need him and that is more than enough for me."

In that moment her steadfast faith in the middle of this organized chaos, confusion and pain in her community, is enough to silence my social theological argument.

"I hear you Mrs. Bridges. You are so right. May I ask you about Samuel Benson?"

"Look Mr. Blume. We gave that boy every chance and then some. My husband and I always treated him with love and respect, loved him like he was one of our own. We knew about his having taken a gun to school but we thought that maybe he was afraid or maybe he needed protection. Come to find, that wasn't the case at all. Most of the kids at the school, if not all of them, were afraid of Samuel!"

"What do you mean? May I put my water down here?" I place my glass on a coaster.

I see Mrs. Bridges take off her apron, fold it neatly and place it on the sofa. She takes a breath and folds her hands almost as if she is trying to keep her composure.

"Samuel…. was selling marijuana and got caught in the bathroom in the middle of a sale. He needed the gun because the school was in another gang's territory."

"He needed the money. Didn't he?"

"Ha! Oh Mr. Blume please. Why? Come on now he

was twelve years old. How much money did he need? His grandparents provided a good home and he never missed a meal. Samuel liked the big boys on the block who drove big fancy cars bought with dirty money, the devil's money! You know what else Mr. Blume the teachers and everybody at school really liked that boy. I mean apart from dealing he never really bothered anybody. He didn't do any of his work in class but he did score high on all the tests they gave him. It's a damn shame that that boy would waste all that God given intelligence."

"That is such a waste of talent Mrs. Bridges. So he gets caught with the gun and he is expelled right?"

"That's right and he was so angry with the school for as he said they were, "getting all up in his business."

I hesitate to ask her why she took this boy into her home. But then I remember what she said about being a fisher of men.

"So you and your husband decide to take the risk and accept him in to your home, knowing that he may be dangerous."

"We all need to be forgiven at some point in our lives. Who else was going to give this boy a chance to get his life together? Besides we thought that maybe getting caught would scare him and he would straighten up."

I see her eyebrows furrow and an intense frown on her face. Her eyes are watery and she starts pausing, taking more time in between each word. "Mrs. Bridges if this is too painful to talk about we can stop."

She puts her hand next to her left cheek and gently

rubs it. Mahalia Jackson singing 'His Eye is on the Sparrow' is playing in the background. Mrs. Bridges takes a few seconds to listen to the lyrics and sings along while looking right at me. I know that I am here to find information so that I can help Samuel but precisely at that moment, by the way that she looks at me while singing those lyrics, I feel the sensation that she is blessing me as I am heading into a storm. She gets back to talking about Samuel.

"You see we really tried to help that boy but the last straw was when he struck me. I was straightening out his room and I could smell the marijuana on his clothes. When I picked up his pants from the floor a big wad of money fell out of the pockets. He came out of the washroom and he saw me standing there with the money in my hand. Then the devil got in that boy and he just lost it. He slapped me and said, "give me my money you stupid old bitch!" I just let him run out of here because if Harold would have found out, then Samuel would not be alive today."

"Mrs. Bridges. I am so sorry that you had to go through something like that. I can't believe that he actually raised his hand to you."

"Believe it son. I told you there is something evil in that boy. He could be kind and sweet but making that fast money was more important to him than anything else."

I didn't know what else to say. I feel like my questions have put this lady through the wringer and I need to put an end to this torturous inquiry.

"Thank you Mrs. Bridges. You have been very helpful."

"Matthew 6:24 you can't have two masters I tell you. A

blind man can see that young Samuel's master is the love of money and all the fancy things he can buy."

I want to tell her that Samuel was no different than corrupt business men and politicians who work in luxurious offices and go to work everyday in a suit and tie. I want to tell her that our society can brainwash people into accepting these values as normal but all I can say is thank you and good bye.

"Thank you for talking with me Mrs. Bridges. I appreciate you taking the time."

"Aren't you forgetting something?"

She goes to the kitchen and comes back with a slice of peach cobbler.

"Take care and be careful getting home Mr. Blume."

"Thank you for the slice of heaven, in more ways than one."

"Oh. I almost forgot. You might want to talk a to Mr. Tyrone Jackson."

"Tyrone Jackson?"

"You can find him at the Black Panther Headquarters in Bed-Stuy. Samuel spent some time with them as well."

"That may be helpful. Thank you again Mrs. Bridges."

I get in my car and start my engine and out of some irrational fear I hesitate about going to Black Panther headquarters. I know exactly where it is and decide that talking to Mr. Jackson may give me more insight on Sam.

Stopped at a red light, I see some kids running and playing tag in a field. Then a man selling snow cones has placed his cart strategically in front of a playground with children pumping their legs on swings to fly up to the sky and going down slides as fast as they can.

After hearing Mrs. Bridges describe what was to her Samuel's fast track to hell, the sound of the children's laughter is quite soothing. All of this feels very inviting so I park my car.

I walk over and ask the man for a snow cone, or by its real name a "piragua."

"Yes sir. You came to the right place. I have the best piraguas in town! What flavor? I got cherry, pineapple, coco.."

"I'll have the coco please."

"Coming right up!"

He took out his metal scraper and starts shaving from the big block of ice on the cart. I love the sound of the ice coming off and making a little mountain on the cone. Then he hits the scraper to get rid of unwanted small pieces of ice, then adds more finer looking crystals. He then takes the coconut flavoring and gracefully pours it around and on top. It cost fifty cents but I give him a dollar for his artistry.

"Thanks young man. Have a great day!"

There are trees calling me to enjoy their shade so I listen to them. The piragua is delicious and the ice feels so good going down. I see a family of three not to far from me.

The father is lying on a low hanging hammock with his legs crossed and covering his face from the sun with his arm. His wife is standing beside him in a black dress and long red hair. It appears that they are having a heartfelt conversation while their baby is sleeping in a stroller besides them.

In the distance I notice another young couple sitting on a blanket. They are looking at each other with their legs stretched out. He is lying on his stomach supporting himself with his elbows while she has her arms out straight behind her and the palms of her hands on the grass. I think that perhaps it is their first or second date and that they are in the process of getting to know each other.

My attention comes back around to my piragua and the many times that I have enjoyed one with pop. Amber knows that I am not looking forward to dinner with him and that's why she reminded me the other night. The tension that has always been there between my father and I from the time I was a boy, has been exacerbated in the three years since mom's death.

I decide to push that to the back of my mind and take in the sights and sounds of people in love, children running and a man selling snow cones. I finish mine, get a drink of water from the fountain then get back in my car and drive to Panther Headquarters.

Traffic is light and I get there in about fifteen minutes. From my car I see two young men with short afros, black berets and green military fatigues, standing perfectly straight. A large black clenched fist is painted on the bricks to the left of the main entrance. Above the door is a sign that reads "Black Panther Party Headquarters, We Serve the People."

"Excuse me gentleman can you please tell me where I can find Mr. Tyrone Jackson?"

"Who's looking for him?"

"I'm Joshua Blume a Social Worker at the Jackson Juvenile Detention Center."

"Come on in and take a seat in front of the receptionist."

He leads me inside and the other man nods and smiles as I walk past him.

"Sister Shirley this is...what did you say your name was?"

"Joshua Blume."

"Mr. Blume a Social Worker over at juvie, he would like to talk with brother Tyrone."

The receptionist calls Tyrone Jackson on the phone, then asks me to come with her. She has on a yellow dress that accentuates her figure with class.

"Brother Jackson's office is the second one on the left."

"Thank you."

On the way to his office I notice a room with two wooden cases mounted on the wall. Each case holds three rifles. Below them there is what appears to be a locked metal military foot locker. Tyrone Jackson reads in my face that I am shaken up a bit at the sight of their weapons.

"Come on in Mr. Blume. Please sit down. You don't have anything to worry about here."

"Do you think that you'll ever need to use those things?" I point in the direction of the weapons in the hall.

"After being in Nam, I hope I never have to again."

"You could achieve your goals without them no?"

"Slavery…., taking a newly born baby from a mother to sell it like some farm animal…., public lynchings while white families enjoyed a picnic lunch, peaceful marchers getting tear gassed and German Shepherds being set loose on them, does this sound like the actions of people who concede power so easily? But then you didn't come here for a history lesson. What's going on man?"

"Samuel Benson. He's serving time at the detention center and I'm trying to help him."

"Good luck. It's sad but that brother may be totally gone."

"Did he work here with you?"

"We had him with us for a couple of weeks. But I couldn't risk him trying to sell pot to these little kids that come here for breakfast or for help with their homework. You know the man is just itching to shut us down. I gave Sam time to change but a hard head makes a soft ass. Know what I mean? Sad I tell you. That boy's a genius! He can do great things if he decides to get his act together."

"I want to help him do just that."

"Yeah you and some detective."

"Detective?"

"He came here a couple of times to talk with Sam. Of course he didn't come inside. He would wait for him across the street."

"How do you know he was a detective."

"The car and cheap suit"

"Well thank you for talking to me, and I hope you never have to open those cases or the foot locker."

"Moses said the same thing before the first Passover. Visit us anytime you like Mr. Blume." His warm welcoming smile made me feel that he truly meant it and wasn't just being polite.

CHAPTER 4

I go back to the office and finish the rest of my paperwork. Before leaving, Maria reminds me that we are having lunch tomorrow at her favorite Chinese place to celebrate her birthday.

On the way home I keep thinking about the depth and strength of Mrs. Bridges. She never has given up on any child before. Could Schmidt have been right about Samuel? Then again who was the detective that Mr. Jackson saw visiting and talking with Samuel? It must have been Schmidt, but why were they even in conversation with each other? These thoughts keep running through my mind until I make it home.

There's Mr. Lerner. He's lifting to be two big boxes, as if they were feathers, and putting them in his trunk.

"Mr. Lerner you certainly didn't need any help with those. I bet you could still bench press about 200 pounds."

"That is funny. Maybe when I was younger, today I am just happy with being able to get them in my car. I am taking it to the Trinity Lutheran Church clothing drive."

I smile at this simple gesture of kindness and wonder

about his motivation. Am I getting to be cynical or is there more than meets the eye? He notices my reaction.

"It is no big deal to get rid of clothes that I am no longer wearing. I do not even consider it generosity."

"You could have just thrown them away or even try to sell them."

"Disposing of it would be a waste and at this point in my life I certainly do not want to waste any of my time haggling with someone over the price of my old shirts."

"I see. Well thanks for reminding me. I need to get some things to them as well."

"I am sure that you were taught the importance of giving as a child. I believe the word is Tzedakah?"

"My mother did her best to pass on the values of her faith. It's another way of saying that it is better to give than to receive."

"Mother only?"

"My father is Puerto Rican and he isn't Jewish."

"Oh. I see. Was your mother's family accepting of your parents' relationship?" As pleasant as he is, I get the sense that Mr. Lerner isn't just being cordial. He is truly interested in what makes me tick.

"Let's just say that the Rosenberg living room became extremely loud when their sweet niece Rebecca came home with Enrique Blume. All this time they were under the impression that Ricky was short for Richard."

"Why were they thinking in such a narrow way?"

"I don't know. I guess that they were just trying to be

protective of their heritage. Strange thing is that maybe my mother being a survivor taught her that love is love."

"Coming from a people who survived senseless destruction that is completely understandable. However, a people need to be careful that their defense does not become a shell of ignorance. Hate is very easily internalized, and in the process can destroy your soul."

"My Arab wife would most certainly agree with you Mr. Lerner."

"Yes? Where is your beautiful wife from?"

"She is Algerian."

"Seems like you go out of your way to make things difficult my friend. Have you thought about bringing peace to the Middle East?"

It is only a figure of speech but when he says "my friend" it makes me feel closer to him. He is completely comfortable talking about killing, prejudice and hatred with a smile and a sense of humor that could put anyone at ease. He continues.

"If people were able to shed their ignorance, there would not be so many wars based on superficial differences of race, or religion."

At that moment Tyrone Jackson's words about people having to struggle and fight sometimes violently, in order to obtain power and just live as free human beings went racing through my mind. Years later I came to realize that at the time I was suppressing outcomes that deep down I knew were inevitable.

"We all could use some slowing down, and thinking

about how we got here and what we really need to do." Wrestling with thoughts that I don't even know are in my mind, is the only thing that allows me to say this.

Mr. Lerner looks down at the ground and touches the back of his head with one hand and lightly rubs his chin and mouth with the other.

"Yes. What needs to be done to right the wrong, right the wrong, right the wrong.......? It was a pleasure talking to you. I have to get to the church. Take care my friend." He gets in to his car and waves good bye.

"You as well Mr. Lerner."

I walk up the stairs and I don't realize how mentally drained I am until I sit down on the sofa. I am feeling sleepy and in the distance I hear the faint sound of Amber's key turning the lock. The last thing I remember before dozing off is Amber's sweet lips kissing me hello. My nap is interrupted way too soon by Danny waking me up for dinner.

"Dad! It's time for dinner."

"That's a switch. Instead of me calling you from the window a thousand times, you're waking me up for dinner. Come here."

I give him a big hug realizing that Danny is about the same age as the look out who I saw on the corner near Mrs. Bridges home.

"You know I love you very much."

"Yeah, I... I... don't get it."

He doesn't understand why I would ask him this question.

"Don't worry champ. I just wanted to tell you. That's all. Did you find any interesting books at the library today?"

"Kind of. I got a book about the Holocaust that seems pretty cool."

"Shoah." I say.

"Huh?"

"Remember your grandmother called it the Shoah."

"Yeah. I forgot."

He picks up the book from the living room table and shows it to me.

"See it has all these cool pictures of soldiers."

"Nazi soldiers, well we can read it together after dinner. Those pork chops smell delicious!"

"Enrique's recipe" Amber said giving full credit to my father.

"The old man is a great cook."

"I heard you two talking about the Shoah. I remember seeing your grandmother almost crying at a dinner party. Her neighbor, Mrs. Rose was sipping on white wine and talking with her about the German composer Wagner. She didn't mean any harm and said holocaust. Remember Josh? Then your mother had to excuse herself and you went to comfort her in the kitchen."

"I remember honey." Then I hear Danny tapping his plate with his fork, and moving the rice from one side to the other.

"You okay champ?" I ask.

"Just thinking about grandma. Maybe I shouldn't have gotten that book."

"Nonsense. You read anything and everything you want. Don't ever feel bad about that. Let's finish eating and then go check out the book together."

"Not so fast Mr. Blume. Don't forget it's your turn to wash the dishes." Amber reminds me.

"I'll help you dad."

"Your pork chops are out of this world mom."

"You don't think that I married your mother just for her looks do you?"

"Well I did marry you for your looks. But your cooking will probably be great tomorrow honey."

I grab Amber and hug her, keeping my hands on the small of her back, feeling the softness of her skin. Prior to having Danny, that alone would have been the start of making love in the kitchen. Instead we go to the living room, sit on the sofa and start looking at the book. Danny is sitting in between us holding the book in his lap.

We look at the open pages of the book and the image of four men in a bunk bed lying on their stomachs with dirt and grime on their faces is hard to see.

"Why are their ribs sticking out so much?", asks Danny.

"They only gave them enough food to barely stay alive and work."

Danny turns the page and is transfixed at the sight of children his age in pin stripe long shirts behind barbed wire fences. Amber turns the page for him. She stops at an image of four Nazi generals in front of a what appears to be a large strong reddish maple desk. In the background is a portrait of Hitler. In the middle of the generals stands a civilian holding blueprints down on the desk.

"Architects, engineers and doctors just "innocently" doing their jobs, helping these monsters, and getting paid nicely." Says Amber.

"Right as always. Look at the general standing to the right of the architect. Does he look familiar?" I ask Amber while thinking about where I have seen this man before.

"No not really"

"It's been a long day. I'm tired. Can we put this away and get some sleep?"

"Yes."

Danny closes the book and kisses us both on the cheek.

"Good night son."

We got ready for bed and I lie to myself. I create a false optimism bout going to work and meeting with Samuel the next day. It takes just about all of my imagination and hope to think that this kid could turn things around. I haven't totally been sold by the nature argument of human behavior but I was no longer blind to the fact that this kid has rejected being nurtured by anybody. He certainly is exercising his free will, knowing that his path has two highly likely destinations, the penitentiary or the graveyard.

Amber is sound asleep, with the notes from her next case in her hand. I take them from her and put them on our night stand. Then I stay in bed with my eyes wide open staring at the cracks in the ceiling. I think about my conversation with Mr. Lerner earlier that evening. Then for some strange reason the image of the Nazi generals and architect from Danny's book come to mind. Lerner was right. The masses are so easily manipulated.

I fall asleep only to be awakened two hours later by the loud ring of the alarm clock.

I get to the office and I see Maria asleep in her chair bent over her typewriter, her black hair touching the keys. She has a wooden plaque of the Puerto Rican flag in the shape of the island on her desk. Her long hoop golden earrings accentuate her multiracial beauty. The Spaniard, Taino and African all come alive in her, in her words she is a true Boricua.

I touch her on the shoulder and she jumps up as if struck by lightning.

"I'm sorry. I just thought that I would wake you up before anybody else saw you cat napping on top of your files."

"Typing up these damn reports is enough to put anyone to sleep."

"Got that right but that's not the reason why you're so tired. Now.... is it?"

"Of course not. We were up all night at the cultural center planning our next activity. We're gonna bring in this great singer and his band from the island."

"That took all night?"

"Are you kidding me? This guy's a piece of work. Man, he's a trip!"

She brings her arms up as if she is holding a guitar.

"A trip?"

"Yeah he sings all these no holds barred songs about independence but then he is so…. bougie. Can't even take a cab or bus. He has to be picked up by a driver at the airport. And the list goes on, and on, and on….."

"Still sounds like an awful long time for planning a show."

She gives me a look and knows exactly what I'm thinking.

"And no, things didn't take so long because I was messing around with Berto. There's no shame in my game. You know that my friend. I'm not afraid of where my decisions can take me. You should try it some time."

"Long live the revolution." I hold up my right hand in a fist.

"That's right, make fun if you want to but when we are free, me, you, Amber and Danny are going to El Yunque."

"Been there remember."

"But this time the water in the river will be even more beautiful and the food will taste even better."

"Fight the good fight Maria."

"I couldn't do this work without being involved in the struggle Josh. This place is a revolving door. As soon as we wrap up a case, there are ten more kids waiting."

"You're right, but then you get kids like Isabel Sanchez. She is about to graduate from the University of Chicago. When only five years ago she was turning tricks at seventeen hooked on heroin."

"No argument from me on that. I love Isabel. But we both know that for every one of her there are one hundred girls still out on those streets. We gotta cut the belly of the beast man, the root of the problem."

"What can I say? Hey, I'm going over to the gym. Samuel Benson's group should be there now."

"That kid gives me a different kind of vibe from the others."

"What do you mean?"

"Be careful. That's all."

"We have to watch ourselves with just about all of these kids."

"This one looks and feels like he knows exactly what he's doing every step of the way. Watch yourself Josh."

I thank Maria for looking out for me and make my way to the gym where Samuel is playing a pick up game of basketball.

I can't believe that kid just slam dunked like Dr J! It's a damn shame how these talented kids end up in a place like this. Why did that guard slip Sam some money?

"Game over suckers!" Says the kid with the emphatic dunk.

The rest of the players are escorted back to their cells by the guards. I wave to them and tell them that I'll take Sam down in a few minutes.

"That was some nice ball playing Sam. We need to talk. Do you have a second?"

"I don't know who 'we'… is, but time is all I got in this place."

He says this while slowly bouncing the ball in perfect rhythm. Then he takes a free throw with tremendous form.

He catches me off guard with a quick chest pass that hits me right in the stomach.

"Let's see what you got."

"It's been a while but I think I can still hit a shot."

My shot makes a loud clunking sound as it hits off of the backboard.

"Guess I'm a little rusty."

He gets the ball and continues his shooting drill.

"I noticed that you get along well with the guards here."

"I can bring out the best in people."

He dribbles the ball in between his legs, while looking at me and smiling. I am pretty sure he knows that I saw the guard give him the money.

"Look you seem like an alright guy, Mr. Blume. It would be better for all of us if you just mind your business."

To a certain degree he was right. Although the thought of not reporting the guard made me uneasy, it might be a better idea to just keep an eye on the situation. I could sense that Sam was reading me and aware of that I was trying to play out this scenario in my mind. Maria was right. This kid was not your average juvenile offender. He was playing the system like a fiddle. He knew from the day he was born that he would flip this wretched system and come out on top.

I see the two old wooden chairs that the guards sit in while the kids play.

"Let's sit down… okay?"

"I rather keep shooting but if it'll make you happy"

He sits down and the smile he has goes away. He intensely looks right at me.

"What was it like volunteering at Black Panther HQ?"

"Why do you want to know?"

"Just wondering. It seems like that would have been a good place for you."

"It was cool and I respect them. When Mr. Jackson asked me to leave, I understood his point. No hard feelings"

"I'm sure Mr. Jackson would have let you stayed if you made a commitment to them."

"Committed will get you in the crazy house baby."

I laugh. Ironically he has a way of putting people at ease.

"Obviously Sam you are extremely intelligent in many ways."

"I know enough to get by."

"You know more than just a little bit to get by."

"So what's the point to all of this? I know you didn't come here to say shit that we both already know."

"Look you're young and have made some serious mistakes, but you're so talented. You don't need the street life. I want to help you."

"With what?"

"Your life, you can't keep doing things like hitting sweet foster mothers who want to help you."

"Mr. Blume" He takes a second and moves his chair just a little closer to mine.

"Yes?"

"The only thing I did wrong was get caught. I don't

make mistakes. I make decisions based on strategic risks. When I slapped Mrs. Bridges it was to teach her old ass a lesson. She needed to learn to not mess with my money."

He sounds so cold and calculating that it sends a shiver down my spine. He stretches out his arms and holds his hands open.

"You see on one hand I could work at the burger joint for minimum wage or I could sell these drugs and make ten times as much money in half the time. See what I mean? I make decisions baby!"

"That fast money comes with a big price Sam."

"Risk, reward baby. That's really what it's all about Mr. Blume. Or should I lie to you and tell you that starting tomorrow, I'm going to change? Either way it doesn't matter. I'll be out of here in no time."

"That may be true but the next time you get busted you won't be sent to Juvie."

"Tell me something I don't know. Have a good day." He gets up and starts walking in the direction of the cells.

"Hold on I have to go back with you."

A guard comes up and takes Sam the rest of the way.

As he walks away from me toward his cell, I am comforted by the fact that he at least talked to me. It wasn't the first time that I had heard a kid talk that way, but he wasn't putting on an act.

My conversation with Sam left me feeling more than a bit empty. I see Maria whistling a non distinct melody while snapping her fingers. Whenever she can she accompanies poets on the bongos during readings at the cultural center.

She has a lovely sense of rhythm but her work here at the office coupled with her activism leaves very little time for anything else.

"Are you ready for Ling's."

"Maria, with the plastic on top of the table cloths and the delicious orange chicken, how could I forget."

"Easily, that's how. Your memory isn't the best these days."

She is right but I honestly hadn't forgotten this time. Maria always has at least one funny story in her. Besides, with being buried in our cases this will give us a chance to relax and talk about things besides work.

"Chicken Chow Mien, here I come. Let's go."

We walk the two blocks to Ling's, and find it a little more busy than normal.

"Hey Ling. How you doing buddy?"

"Blume you know better than to show up with this Yankee fan." Ling points at Maria with a mock scowl on his face.

"Blume, is proud to be with this Yankee fan" Maria says.

"Well my beloved Sox are still the best."

"We'll see my friend."

Ling drops the baseball fan rivalry banter and puts on his warm welcoming smile."Birthday girl, your table is waiting."

"You remembered Ling?"

"You have your boy here Blume to thank for that. He called ahead just to make sure."

"Thanks Josh."

Ling shows us to our table and then goes back to the bar area and sits on his black stool right next to the phone. He doesn't sell liquor but he takes delivery orders from the bar, and he moves gracefully with his wiry frame to take care of the customers sitting at the tables. From time to time he will go in to the kitchen only to get kicked out by the corpulent cook, who wants no advice on how to prepare the food.

We don't need to look at the menus, of course. Maria loves their shrimp fried rice. Even though the place was small and only had six tables, the wall mirrors give the dining area the illusion of having more space.

"This is for you my friend. Happy Birthday to my favorite Boricua!"

"You know that I'm going to open it right now." She unwraps the gift in one second. "Usmail, thanks Josh!"

I had remembered that she had somehow lost her copy of the Pedro Juan Soto novel two weeks ago.

"Does that mean that the old, always present Josh is back?"

"Maybe, let's hope so. So tell me all about your trip to Puerto Rico with Berto. Did you love it?"

"You know that I love being there with all my heart. Berto... not as much."

"You've been together now for just about a year no? Trouble in paradise?"

"No. Man..for that to be true you have to have paradise in the first place. Don't get me wrong Josh. I like him and all but somethings not quite clicking. Know what I mean? We could be in deep conversation about Brecht and his plays, or Gutierrez's liberation theology and we start connecting on an intellectual level with which I can't do without. But then we start kissing and zero, nada, I'm just not feeling it Josh!"

"Sometime those intangible sweet subtle sensations can't be found."

"You're telling me. It's a big red flag when you're walking hand in hand at night on the beach at Isla Verde with the moon shimmering off of the water and the breeze slightly cooling you off and all you can think about is the lobster stuffed mofongo that you had for dinner."

"Maria, in spite of the lack of connection with Berto, all of that sounds so beautiful."

"You know me Josh. Even though I was born here every time that I go back, it feels like home to me. Man my grandmother cooked this fresh chicken soup. Woooo! And when I say fresh, I mean go to the backyard, get one of the chickens and chop off its head. That's fresh man!"

"I guess Jewish mothers aren't the only ones making chicken soup."

"Tell me how are things with you and Amber?"

"Let's just say that Amber has her own special way of making sure that I stay attentive."

Sitting diagonally from us are five university seminary students. They were having a conversation about how much they love their urban mission. I looked at Maria and immediately knew what she was thinking.

"Don't get me wrong Josh. They're probably great kids but, we don't need saviors, we need allies!"

"I hear you loud and clear Maria." I look over her shoulder and see Ling coming our way. Hey here comes our food."

"Here we go; four egg rolls, chicken chow mien and shrimp fried rice"

"Thanks Ling you're the best."

"You're alright too, for a Yankee fan."

The food is delicious as always. We might be here celebrating Maria's birthday but the couple of hours spent laughing and distracted, are good for me as well. The time goes by in a flash and we make our way back to the office.

CHAPTER 5

After filling out the one millionth report for the same incident I am looking forward to getting home, to our sanctuary. I want to know if Danny got his two homers playing stickball. The warmth in Amber's arms is also calling me. Those peaceful images begin to shatter like broken glass when I drive up to our building and see her crying next to a parked ambulance, in front of a crowd with concerned faces combined with onlookers who want their mundane day broken up with some excitement.

She sees me and immediately runs up to me and hugs me intensely.

"No time to talk. Danny's in the ambulance. I'll ride with him and you can meet us there."

"Where?" I ask.

"St. Anthony's"

I am about to get in my car when Mr. Lerner walks over to me and puts his hand on my shoulder.

"Please let me know how the boy is doing when you return. I got to him as fast as I could."

He notices the confused look on my face.

"Go, go. Your wife will explain."

At the hospital the receptionist tells me that Danny is being seen in the emergency room, only as a precautionary measure.

Amber comes toward me from behind a set of doors and tells me, "They just started checking out his lungs."

"What happened? He had his inhaler didn't he?"

"He did. But this happened so fast. I got home from work and the boys were playing like they do every day. I waved to him, and he smiled. I went upstairs into our place and threw my briefcase on the sofa then took out the seasoned lamb from the refrigerator and started making dinner. Then all of a sudden I noticed that it was so quiet. The usual sounds of kids running or arguing over the score of the game had stopped, so I looked out the window. That's when I saw all of them huddled around something or someone. When I got downstairs, I saw that it was Danny in the middle of the crowd. He was sitting and Mr. Lerner was holding his head, telling him to breathe slowly and giving him sips of coffee. Little David told me that Danny had had an attack. He couldn't find his inhaler in time and started coughing and convulsing uncontrollably. They all said that Mr. Lerner was watching and practically flew to help Danny. Thank goodness that somebody called an ambulance and they got there right away."

Tears came to both of us from the thought of Danny clutching his chest and not being able to take in any air.

"Mrs. Blume?"

"Yes Dr., Dr. Hudson this is my husband Josh."

"Pleased to meet you Dr. Hudson."

"Danny'll be fine. We'll keep him overnight just to make sure that he's alright. You can go in and see him now, room 213."

"Thank you Dr."

In the room we see Danny lying listlessly on his bed. Amber gently takes his hand and kisses his head.

"How are you feeling sweetie?"

"I hit two homers."

"Two?! Did you hear that Josh?"

"You bet I heard that, just like Reggie!"

"Yeah. I can hit just like him right dad?"

"That's right champ."

"Can I have some chocolate ice cream mom?"

"As soon as we get home tomorrow. They want you to stay overnight. I'll be right here with you."

"Just don't tell the guys mom. I don't want them thinking I'm a scaredy cat."

"Don't worry about it kiddo. Besides who cares what they think? You're a big strong boy who can handle himself. Don't ever worry about what people think." Amber reassures him.

"Thanks mom." Danny curls up closer to Amber who is sitting on the bed.

Seeing Danny being comforted by Amber makes me feel so much better. "I'm going home. I want to thank Mr. Lerner, before it gets any later. Hey champ, make sure to take good care of your mom tonight."

"I will dad."

"See you in the morning."

I kiss Amber and start walking out of the room.

Just as I am leaving, a paramedic walks in.

"It's good to see that your boy is better. I'm Ismael Perez. My partner and I were called to the scene today when he got sick. We got lucky that old man knew that coffee would help him."

"We're very fortunate to have a neighbor like Mr. Lerner. Aren't we Josh?"

"Yeah. Well, he gave us this. Said it belonged to your boy."

He hands me a medal with an eagle's head and a swastika in the middle.

"This isn't Danny's." I look at in disbelief.

"The old man said that it fell out of your boy's pocket. It's yours now. Maybe you can ask him about it?"

Amber takes it from my hand. "Why do you think he would have something like this?"

"Maybe he's a collector of some kind. I don't know. It might not even be his."

The paramedic shrugs. "Well I'm glad your son is ok. You folks have a good night."

"Thank you Mr. Perez."

The images of the Nazi generals in Danny's book, my aunt dying in a gas chamber with dozens of other lifeless bodies at her feet, and the thought of this eagle with a swastika on it possibly belonging to Mr. Lerner, are spinning on a merry go round in my mind, as I am driving home from the hospital.

Then I vividly remembered the sound of my mother summoning enough energy to be able to speak in a whisper. My sisters and I there listening to her about the people who even up to the last second of life, believed that water was going to come out of the shower head.

I am so distracted by this that my car comes to a screeching stop when I come down hard on the brake. A kid had turned the corner on his bike and I am so deep in thought that I almost didn't see him in time.

When I get home and park, there is Mr. Lerner sitting on his front steps calm, cool and collected as always.

"Mr. Blume. I take it that your son is going to be fine."

"He will. They are just going to keep him overnight. I can't thank you enough Mr. Lerner. Thank you for being there for him."

"You really want to show me your gratitude?"

I don't really quite understand his question. He notices, smiles and puts me at ease.

"Please come in for some coffee."

"Thank you. A little relaxation and coffee sounds good right about now."

I walk into his home. The hardwood floors are incredibly shiny. There isn't a speck of dust on his book shelves and mantle. The rippled curtains flow elegantly to the floor.

"Whatever your cooking it smells delicious."

"Beef stew. Please feel free to stay for dinner."

He walks to the kitchen but I stay in the living room.

I see a family portrait hanging on the wall above a piano. In it is a handsome man in a three piece suit who looks very familiar but I can't place him. He is standing above a stunning smiling woman who is looking down at the baby she is holding in her arms. Next to them is a beautiful girl in pig tails about five years old. She is also looking at the baby with her mouth open expressing pure delight.

He comes back in with two cups of coffee.

"I added a little cream and sugar. Hope you like it?"

"That's fine thank you." I say. Taking the cup I gesture toward the piano. "Do you play? I've never heard any sounds coming from your window."

"Only when I am incredibly happy."

"That's a beautiful portrait."

"Thank you. That was close to the end. For my boy it was his first and last year of life."

"That's incredibly sad Mr. Lerner. May I ask what happened?"

"They were murdered. Casualties of war in the Allies Bombing of Berlin."

I am struggling for words to say. All I can do is look at him.

"No need to be sorry if you feel that their death was a necessary evil."

"I don't feel that way Mr. Lerner."

"You do believe that Hitler needed to be stopped at all costs no? But we don't need to continue talking about this. By the way that you looked at me when you came out of your car I don't think that you came to talk to me about how my family was killed."

"Come now Mr. Blume please sit."

"You're right and it should have been the first thing I said. My wife and I want to let you know how grateful we are for saving Danny today."

"I have absolutely no doubt that you would have done the same for me Mr. Blume. I trust you to be a man who will do the right thing when the time comes."

"I try to but it doesn't get any easier with time." I wonder what he means by that.

"I can assure you that it won't either. Especially for someone such as yourself who wants to contribute to righting the wrongs of the world."

He says this in a very intentional way. Not only was I dealing with a crooked cop and a highly intelligent kid with a penchant for slapping kind and loving foster mothers at work, now I had to face the reality that the very man who saved my son's life was a Nazi general during WW2. God if there is your way of testing me please let me know. He looked at me and read me like a book.

"You have something that belongs to me do you not?"

Mr. Lerner puts his cup down on the table.

"Yes I do."

I slowly take the medal out of my pocket, reach to the other side of the table and give it to him. He holds it in his hand, smiles and then I pick up what I think is a sigh of relief.

"Yes Mr. Blume. I am who you think I am."

I look at the family portrait again. "That is you! The other day my son and I were looking at a book that he brought home from the library. I saw a man and I thought of you, perhaps when you were younger."

"It could have been me, posing for pictures of a dark time that doesn't need to be remembered."

"My aunt was murdered in a gas chamber."

"And my wife and children along with 400,00 German civilians served as "collateral damage", killed by the allied forces. I have had much more than my fair share of intimate encounters with death. Yet I know that life is precious."

"The way you saved my son I believe you."

"Losing a child is a tragedy that I would not wish upon my worst enemy."

"And yet you were part of a system, check that, a high ranking decision maker, of a carefully designed genocidal machine. You helped plan the death of six million people. How does that factor in to not wanting to see your enemy lose his child?"

"Those people weren't my enemy. They were part of a job, a task that had to be done. It's like going to work, sitting at your desk and working on files, nothing more nothing less. Please know that not a day goes by without me thinking about the blood on my hands. But I am not alone Mr. Blume. All of our hands are soiled by this mess we call humanity and society."

"I suppose that saving Danny's life helped you wash away some of that blood."

As he speaks he turns and looks up at his family portrait.

"I know how much you love your family. Today when

your boy went down and was gasping for air like a fish out of water, I saw my own child."

"When you were a Nazi general didn't you see your own children in the faces of those being slaughtered?"

"I did but I was also working for the good of my children. Just as the Allied soldiers who killed innocent civilians did. Yet we were all so tragically wrong."

He sits back in his chair, takes a deep sigh, puts his face in between his hands and starts to cry. He stops and while he is drying his face with a handkerchief from his shirt pocket, his look penetrates my very soul.

"Now you know who I really am Mr. Blume. What will you do?"

"I wish I knew. I wish that I knew. Good night Mr. Lerner."

Mr. Lerner's revelation was the culmination of a horrific day. I barely have enough energy to walk across the street to our apartment. On automatic pilot I open the door, throw the keys on the living room table and sit on our sofa. All I can do is sit and stare out into a world that is moving too fast for me. My mind and body shut down and out of mental exhaustion. I fall asleep.

CHAPTER 6

"Mommy, mommy, mommy! Can't you hear me?! Mommy! Please don't go! Come back!" I am screaming loudly.

"Josh wake up. Wake up honey." Amber grabs me by the arms and shakes me.

"Huh, oh……. I'm sorry Amber."

"It's okay. What were you dreaming?"

"About me and my mom. I guess I was about five years old and we were crossing the street to a park. She held me by the hand so tightly." Amber sees me rubbing my hand as if I am trying to bring back the circulation. I can see that she is worried and I continue talking about my dream.

"Children were running, chasing each other and laughing. They were going back and forth on the swings pumping their legs to fly as high as possible. It was winter and everybody had a coat on but mom. A Black man in green fatigues was enjoying a hot dog that he had just gotten from a vendor then walked over to an Asian woman who hugged and kissed him before taking a bite."

"They were part of your dream?"

"Yeah. Then mom was looking at two little girls jumping

rope. One of them had on a green dress with daisies and the other a pink dress with red flowers. I looked up at mom and saw that she was crying tears of joy. I don't ever remember seeing her that happy. I called her and she looked down at me while letting go of my hand. She didn't answer me, and went back to watching the girls. Then the three of them started drifting farther and farther away from me, but I couldn't even move when I tried running towards them. I kept calling her and It didn't matter how loud I screamed or how many times I tried. She wouldn't answer me, didn't even look my way."

Amber hugs me bringing me back into the present. "I wonder why you had such a strange dream with all of those different people. You still have your clothes on from yesterday. You slept all night like that?"

"I was so wiped and fell asleep the second I sat down. What time is it?"

"Time to get ready for work. But maybe you should take a day and get some rest."

"I'll be alright. How's Danny?"

"He's more than fine. I just came to take a shower before I head back to the hospital. He'll be discharged at about noon. Would you like to go with me? Maybe the three of us can grab a bite somewhere?"

"And miss Schmidt bringing me more clients? Can't do that." I get up and try to stretch out the soreness from having slept all night sitting down. I walk to the kitchen and pick up the newspaper. The headline wakes me right up like cold water splashed on my face.

Amber sees me holding the paper. I don't know what to make of the headline.

"Nine injured in bombing of the Mechanic and Traders Bank. Puerto Rican Independence Movement takes credit."

"I saw that. By the way you're looking at it, seems like you and Maria will have a lively discussion today."

Once again my automatic pilot kicks in and all I can tell Amber is that the coffee taste a little bitter. She doesn't even bother to answer. Letting me know that if I want it to be different, I would have to make it myself.

I get dressed without noticing or even caring that I am wearing different color socks. I swallow some cereal, walk out of our place and get in the car. A former Nazi general saving my son's life, the morning's headline, along with all the other complications at work, are the thoughts swirling in my mind. When I get to the office, I walk right past Maria. I am trying to suppress my deep inner thoughts caused by the whirlwind of the last two days. I know that this is not the time to argue with Maria.

"Hey! What's up Josh? You don't want to be seen talking to me?" Maria comes right at me.

"Don't be ridiculous. Nice t-shirt by the way." I say to her.

"That's right. ¡Que Viva Puerto Rico Libre! Supporting those who fight for freedom is not a crime." Maria lets me know that she is not about to hide her convictions, even if it made some people uncomfortable.

"Tell that to the mothers, wives, fathers and sons who are going to visit their loved ones at hospitals today, Maria!"

"No problem. Then I'll take them to talk with women who fell in love and wanted to have babies but surprise, they couldn't because come to find out, they were sterilized without even knowing it. And while we're at it I can introduce them to the heroin addicts who just wanted for a minute to escape a world that tells them on a consistent basis that being inferior is their birthright. Tell me Josh what other gifts of colonialism can I share with them?"

"A lot of change is going to come from bombing a bank isn't it Maria? Please tell me that you don't know the people who did this."

"Josh you're much smarter than that my friend. I couldn't tell you even if I did."

She comes from behind her desk and walks up to me. Then she puts her hand next to my head as if she was holding a gun.

"You're telling me that if you could blow the head off of one of those Nazis who killed your aunt, your mother's sister, you wouldn't do it?"

"Why do you ask me that?"

"Just answer. Don't think."

"Justice would have to be done."

She takes her hand away from my head, goes back to her desk and sits down.

"That's not what I asked you. But don't worry, I still love you."

I sit down at my cluttered desk and see three messages next to my phone.

"These are all from Mrs. Bridges?"

"Yeah. She called yesterday and I could barely make out what she was saying, she was talking so fast."

"I'm going to see what's going on with her. Thanks Maria."

I turn to see the police bringing in three Black boys all about the age of 13. I can see the tight handcuffs cutting off their circulation. All of them had on expensive jeans and short sleeve silk shirts. A cold hardness was etched into their eyes, their innocence completely gone.

I sat down and call Mrs. Bridges. She picks up the phone on the very first ring and I can hear the fear in her voice. She talks in a stunted way.

"Mrs. Bridges? Joshua Blume here. You called three times yesterday. Sorry that I'm just getting back to you today."

"I am so sorry Mr. Blume but I just didn't know who else to call."

"No need to apologize. You can call me anytime."

"I, I...."

I look over at the three boys being processed and one of them sticks up his middle finger in a defiant tone.

"Hey, I'm not the enemy kid!"

"Enemy?"

"I'm sorry Mrs. Bridges. I was talking to a kid here."

"Can you please come to my house? I need to talk to you."

"What happened?"

"Please Mr. Blume."

"I'm on my way Mrs. Bridges."

I hang up the phone and look at the falling rain. It is so light that it barely makes any sound when it hits the window. It slowly slides down leaving behind little tiny bubbles. And for a brief second I get lost in the world of this water that has no choice but to come down to earth and finish its transformation, just so that it can start it all over again.

Not only am I living with the reality that the man who saved my son's life is a former Nazi general, now I have to contend with Maria surfacing thoughts that I did not want to face. If she was involved in any way with an armed independence movement did I resent her for at least having the courage to face evil and take direct action? How committed was I really to these kids who go round and round on this dizzying carousel, in and out of jail as if they were coming to only visit old friends? The sound of these thoughts was becoming so loud that I started developing a lingering dull pain in my head. Did Mr. Lerner make his hideous confession because he wanted his suffering to come to an end? Was he tired of living a lie? After my visit with Mrs. Bridges, I realize that things are about to get much more complicated or simplified depending on how you look at it.

By the time that I leave the office the light drizzle has turned into a full storm. I cover my head with a newspaper and run to my car. The paper didn't help much as the strong wind makes sure that my clothes become drenched.

CHAPTER 7

As I get closer to Mrs. Bridges' home I look to my right and see a beautiful Black woman wearing a faded soiled jean jacket with a red bandana wrapped around her head. She is walking the streets and looking in to car windows letting the drivers know that she is selling sexual favors. Looking at her reminds me of a study I read once on the use of methadone to treat intravenous heroin addicts. One of the participants was a woman who was making up to two hundred dollars a day selling her body on the street. She would spend every cent of it to maintain her and her husband's heroin addiction. In her words the poor woman said she would do anything to keep her husband from; "feelin' sick." Inner City Blues is playing on someone's radio, making the scene seem surreal.

I drive a few more blocks and park in front of her home. I ring her bell and Mrs. Bridges immediately opens the door.

"Please come in Mr. Blume. Thank you for coming to see me."

She is visibly shaking. I look up at the painting of the Last Supper and a sense of dread that the worse is yet to come, is the only feeling that it provokes in me. Strength and poise to meet one's demise with dignity and grace is something that I am going to need in the coming days.

"I just finished brewing a fresh pot of coffee. Would you like some?"

"Thank you Mrs. Bridges."

She comes back and I can hear the sound of the cup against the dish as she is walking.

"What's wrong? I've never seen you like this Mrs. Bridges"

"I don't want you to get in any trouble, but I just don't know who else I can call."

"Don't worry about me. Please tell me what happened to have you looking like this. I know you don't scare easily."

As a child, Mrs. Bridges had seen her fair share of cross burnings in Mississippi, yet her faith has kept her strong. So whatever has her in this state must have been horrific.

"That man came here today."

"What man?"

"That so called civil servant, Detective Schmidt, was here."

"That's no big deal. I'm sure he came here because he's working on Samuel's case."

"Oh, he's working on the case alright."

"What do you mean?"

"Look Mr. Blume, you just need to watch your back."

"Why would I need to do that?" I take a sip of my coffee and do my best to remain calm for Mrs. Bridges.

"He came and banged on my door so hard, it sounded like he was going to break it down. I managed to have that fool ease up a little bit and he took a seat on the sofa. He asked me politely if I knew that Samuel had something that belonged to him. Of course I didn't know what he was talking about. Then a complete rage took over his body. He got up grabbed me by my blouse and pulled me close enough to his stinking mouth, then whispered to me. I can still feel his hot breath on my neck. He told me that he had already killed so many niggers on the street and and that me and my husband would just be two more. Oh dear lord I can't believe that demon just made me say that word!"

Mrs. Bridges began crying. I try to reassure her by putting my arm around her.

Then she gives me a hug as if she is also consoling me.

"Mr. Blume please don't deal with that man by yourself."

"Don't worry. Please don't even give this another thought. He is just fishing for information. He won't touch you. I will be fine."

"He warned me not to tell anybody, especially you."

"That sounds like Schmidt alright. Of course he wouldn't want me to know about this."

"He said something about you taking up for Samuel. What really worried me was the way he talked about your wife and child."

"My family? What did he say about Amber and Danny?"

"He said that he would hate to see anything bad happen to them on account of your work."

"He's all talk. Don't you worry about a thing Mrs. Bridges. This is all going to be over soon."

For a brief second I have a feeling of clarity unlike any I had felt in my life. Any ambiguity goes totally out the window when it comes to protecting Danny and Amber. Although in reality it is really just Danny as Amber is more than capable of dealing successfully with any harm that may come her way.

I thank Mrs. Bridges as I get back in my car to make it back home.

I get there at 6 and walk in the door. Amber is dressed in her beautiful blue midi dress. It was at that point that I remember that my father had gotten her that dress last year for her birthday. When it comes to women, he has always been very thoughtful. One day, two weeks before her birthday, while walking with her and Danny he noticed Amber looking through the department store window. He knew exactly what she was looking at and made a mental note, while saying absolutely nothing to her.

Amber knows that I have forgotten our dinner plans the moment I walk in the door.

"You forgot that we're having dinner at your dad's tonight didn't you?"

Between dealing with the Schmidt situation at work and Lerner's morbid revelation, it had completely slipped my mind.

"Yes I did."

"Well hurry up Josh. You know he hates it when people are late."

"Get off my back will you! Why are you so worried about what he doesn't like?"

"What is wrong with you? I'm just trying to make sure that the evening gets off to a good start that's all. And that's why I'm going to ignore that last comment. Now please go get ready."

In a moment of ignorant defiance I walk over to the refrigerator and grab a cold beer that has been there for maybe six months. I don't even like beer but I take a sip and surprisingly find it a bit refreshing in the eighty - five degree heat. In a desperate attempt to maintain a sense of control I drink about half then threw the rest away in the sink.

"Are you done?"

"Yes I am. I need a shower."

Danny comes out of his bedroom and I kiss him on the forehead as I pass him and walk straight to the bathroom. I take off my clothes in front of the mirror as I ask myself why I would pull such a ridiculous macho stunt. I consider myself above that type of behavior but lately I find myself reacting as opposed to thinking. Worse than that when I finish showering and dressing, I don't even apologize to Amber and that adds to the tension once we get to my father's.

CHAPTER 8

Pop hasn't lost his touch. I can smell the fried pork chops from the moment we walk into the home of Mr. Enrique Blume. He opens the door and there we are standing. Danny is in his brown shorts and matching polo. Amber is wearing her beautiful dress and me with my jeans and black t-shirt. My father would forgive Danny for wearing shorts because he is a kid. But I notice the subtle disapproving look that he gives me when he sees my outfit. Nevertheless he manages to summon that warm and welcoming smile of his.

"Hi Pop. Bendición."

"Dios te bendiga mijo."

"Bendición abuelo."

"Dios te bendiga. Come here let me give you a big hug. Uuumph I love this boy sooo much. Come on put them up. Lemme see that old one - two. Just like I showed you."

My father has Danny go in to a boxing stance and holds up his hands so that he can hit him.

"Pop, what are you doing? We talked about this remember?"

"You talked about it. I just heard you. Come on sometimes a man's gotta know how to defend himself." He drops the impromptu boxing lesson to focus on Amber.

"And there she is. Stunning as always. Where did you get that dress? It looks lovely on you." He gracefully walks to her and kisses her cheek.

"I love it thank you Enrique! And your cooking smells delicious as always!"

"Yes it does. But I can't claim that tonight Amber. Wanda took care of preparing dinner."

"Wanda? Do you have something to tell us?" I ask.

Amber and I are caught a little off guard. It has been five years since mom died. Until then pop has been pretty much alone.

"Wanda." "Wandaaa, come here mi amor." Wanda comes in from the kitchen wearing a red blouse and an apron tied around a flowered print skirt.

"Wanda this is my son Josh, his adorable wife Amber and that handsome young man, is my grandson Danny. Everybody say hello to Wanda, my new girlfriend."

"Who in the world has a new girlfriend at the age of 70?" I whisper into Amber's ear.

"Not now Josh. You're going to embarrass her. We can talk about it later."

Ordinarily I would have been happy for my father. But that isn't the case on this night.

"Hello Josh. It's good to meet you. Your father has told me so much about you."

"That makes one of us. Why have you been keeping this a secret pop?"

"Well it's not a secret son. I just wanted to tell you and have you meet her all at the same time. That way I don't have to hear the same questions asked over and over. You can get to know her and ask everything that you want right here tonight."

"Well I for one think that it's great Enrique."

"Thank you Amber."

"Danny say hello to Wanda."

"Danny. You are a handsome boy! Enrique was right. Do you have a girlfriend?"

"Girlfriend? He's only ten." I say to Wanda.

"Take it easy Josh. You had a girlfriend when you were ten. Remember that skinny girl who lived across the street? What was her name, a, a Diana!"

"Diana was not my girlfriend pop."

"Okay. That's why you were always looking out the window to see if she was in front of her house and then, went outside running as soon as you saw her. Didn't you?"

My father imitates me as a little boy running to his first crush, with eyes wide open and arms and legs pumping fast. He has always been quite the story teller.

"Tell us Wanda how did you two meet?"

"At Silver Sneakers Amber. I had seen him around for about two weeks. I noticed that I caught his eye but he was a perfect gentleman! He didn't come rushing at me like a bull in a china shop." Wanda elegantly takes a couple of steps over to my father and places her hand on his heart.

"That's right. I took my time. That's just the way my negrita likes it." They share a little peck on the lips.

"Okay!!! Let's eat. I'm hungry." I say to interrupt my dad's amorous remarks.

We take our places at the dinner table.

As we are passing the food around my father continues the conversation. "Hey Amber the other night we were watching Ed Sullivan and these hippies were on singing. Now they weren't half bad but I couldn't get over the way they were dressed! When musicians go on stage they need to be dressed right. You would never see Sinatra or Tito Rodriguez singing without their suit and tie. Now that's class."

"If you don't approve of what I have on just tell me." I said to my father.

"No need to, you know I don't like it."

"Did you cook the arroz con gandules too Wanda?"

Wanda looked at Amber and her voice wavers a bit as she can sense the growing tension between my father and I.

"Yes my dear. I cooked it all."

"One day I'm going to master that dish." Replies Amber.

"I'll be more than happy to help you. Just let me know when." Wanda says with sincerity.

My father gets up and walks over to Wanda. He had begun dancing at a very early age and he was smooth as silk. When they were young, he loved swinging to the Mambo of Tito Puente at the Palladium with my mother. I remember the pictures and they made a beautiful couple.

By the way he glides over to Wanda's side of the table, I can see that he hasn't lost his touch. He kisses her softly on her cheek, showing his appreciation to Wanda for being kind and warm to us. She blushes and almost turns the color of her blouse. The pearl necklace around her neck gives her a dignified look. But I am so blinded by my irrational anger that I decide to ignore any kind of compliment that I can think of for her. I knew that showing up to dinner in a pair of jeans and a t-shirt would not sit well with my father at all. It was as if I wanted to upset him and I was begging for a fight.

"What do you think of the food son?"

"It's alright."

"Just alright?"

"It taste good but it could use just a bit of salt."

"Josh."

"Why are you Joshing me Amber?"

"I'm so sorry I forgot the salt. Us older folks have to watch our blood pressure." Wanda says joking, and no one laughs.

"Is there something wrong? You've seemed a little off from the moment you walked in the door." My father can tell that I have something heavy on my mind. For a second he is willing to put macho posturing aside.

"He has been having a rough time at work lately. Enrique."

"I'm alright pop. Im just dealing with an extremely difficult situation at work."

"You can handle it. Just don't let the pressure make you mess things up."

"Now what is that supposed to mean?"

"Nothing son. Eat your food."

"Hey abuelo. Are you coming to my summer camp basketball game next week? You haven't come to any games this year."

"He's probably been too busy at Silver Sneakers." I say.

"I'll be there kiddo." Answers my father while looking at me to let me know that he heard me and that he is just going to ignore my comment.

Poor Wanda. I can tell that she was aware of the uneasy exchange between my father and I. It is making her uncomfortable. For the rest of dinner we eat in silence and you can cut the tension with a knife. Mercifully dinner comes to an end. Then Wanda and pop serve us chocolate ice cream for dessert, and in an attempt to lighten the atmosphere, Amber suggests eating it in the living room. We walk over to the living room and Danny sits on the sofa. He looks up at the mantel and sees my 7th grade class picture to the right of my father's old chime clock.

"Hey dad who are those kids in that school picture?"

"That's your father's 7th grade picture. You see that big kid in the back row, the first one on the left? That's Jimmy Robinson." My father says before I have a chance to answer.

I haven't thought of Jimmy, and what happened to him, for more than twenty years.

"Who's Jimmy Robinson."

"Nobody Danny. Forget about it. Your grandfather is just talking. That's all."

"Don't be shy Josh. Jimmy Robinson was the class bully. I don't know how many times he had taken your dad's lunch money. Then one day your dad-"

"Wanda. Where are you from again?"

"Not good to interrupt your old man son. Why are you all of the sudden so interested in her?"

My father knows that I have chosen to forget this episode in my life but he insists on telling Danny the story.

"I tell you Danny one day your father was walking across the playground on his way home after school. Jimmy Robinson came up to him with two other boys. Jimmy told him; "Hey Blume you forgot to give me your lunch money today." That day your father had decided that he wasn't going to take it no more. And just like that boom, he hit Jimmy right between the eyes with his history book. The kid didn't even see it coming and he was knocked out before he hit the ground. For good measure Josh hit him one time and Jimmy started bleeding from his mouth. An ambulance had to be called for Jimmy."

"Wow dad! That's cool!"

"No Danny. That's not cool." I turn to my father.

"What is wrong with you! Why would you tell him that story?!"

"Now be careful Josh. I'm an old man but don't you forget who's the father here. Why are you so upset? That little punk had it coming to him!"

"Amber, let's go!"

"Enrique, Wanda I'm so sorry."

"No need to apologize! Let's get out of here!"

Wanda reaches out to touch Amber on her arm and says; "Please, please stay."

"Let them go Wanda. Can't teach my grandson how to box or talk about how his old man finally stood up for himself. I'm just being me in my house, nothing wrong with that."

"I'm sorry we can come back some other time." Says Amber and we leave.

The silence in the car is deafening. Danny has fear in his eyes from seeing his father angrily raise his voice at his mother. While driving I continued arguing with Amber.

"I can't believe that you encouraged that ridiculous behavior from him!"

"What are you talking about?"

"Well I don't know, let's start with his new girlfriend."

"Would you prefer for your father to be a bitter old man, alone and lonely? Your mother has been gone for five years now."

"No. Of course not, but he has his dominoes group."

"They play once a week and you know that a woman's tender company can't even begin to compare to his cigar smoking, beer belching buddies. Josh have you thought about getting back in the pool more often? It could help you with this stress that has you all worked up."

"Now that's a low blow Amber!"

"Low blow? I'm just trying to help."

She looked at me tenderly touched my stomach which

75

was a bit larger those days. Amber was trying to bring levity to the situation by joking about it, but I was incapable of taking it that way. She started saying;

"You know that a little swimming wouldn't...."

"I knew it! I saw that look on your face when you saw me in my t-shirt today!"

"Dad why are you yelling at mom? What's wrong?"

"Tell him Josh. Tell our son why you're so upset."

I can't. I am so wrapped up in my thoughts that any attempt to explain my actions would be futile. It has gotten to the point where the conflicting emotions of fear and having the courage needed to do what is right and just, has taken over my mind. Pop telling that Jimmy Robinson story had me asking myself if I was a coward who only talked about justice but was incapable of taking any action. At that moment, as much as I tried I could not stop hearing the words from the God of retribution in my mother's holy scriptures.

The next morning I wake up to Amber staring at me from the edge of the bed, standing fully dressed in her pant suit ready to be a no nonsense public defender. I know that I was wrong for my actions and for talking to her the way that I did but all I could say is good morning.

"Good morning honey."

"The next time the thought of raising your voice to me crosses your mind, especially in front of Danny, you better think again."

"I know it's just that....... I don't know. I'm sorry. I just wasn't in the right frame of mind to meet my father's new girlfriend or to reminisce over schoolyard bullies."

"You're going to be late for work."

I get up from underneath the blanket and sit down. She stands in front of me and takes my face in her hands. "Tell me did you have another episode like the other day when you almost lost it and cried uncontrolably?"

"No, it's just that when I think about people like Maria and Tyrone Jackson"

"Tyrone who?" Amber asked.

"Jackson. I met him the other day at Black Panther Headquarters."

"You must have gone there for one of your kids."

"Yeah, to learn more about Samuel Benson. Like I was saying, the people there, just like Maria seem to be so decisive and know the actions that they need to take. I don't always agree with them but.."

"They have a little more skin in the game." Amber pointed out a reality that perhaps I had lost sight of. Lately things were hitting too close to home for me. It was becoming crystal clear that events were happening, causing me to lose my privilege as only an interested participant.

"For that matter even you honey, you worked that Mullins' case with no hesitation." I say.

"You know me. When I'm in the dojo sparring against an opponent, I love her like a sister, but the moment she tries to attack I'm going to take her head off."

"Not everyone's a black belt Amber."

"No need to be honey. Mullins was a vulture, always circling to eat what he thought was already dead. When that happens, show people that you're alive and defend what you love, who you love."

She walks out with Danny and I can hear the sound of the lock as she turns the key. I stayed sitting in bed thinking about the revolving door at work that brings in 12 and 13 year olds already hardened by their day to day existence living in a world in which they are exploited by those who are suppose to mentor and love them, but instead make them ready to sell anything or kill anyone. Then I vividly remember my conversation with Tyrone Jackson. When rightfully so he let me know that under no uncertain terms was he going to allow his people to be slaughtered like innocent lambs. His words about the first Passover and the Exodus being bloody acts of resistance that are now holy days ring so true. Like rapid fire, Maria's challenge to me as to what I will do when my moment of truth arrives, kept hitting my consciousness, like a runaway train these thoughts kept moving and gained a life of their own when Mr. Lerner's revelation came into the mix. Why reveal his crimes and his suffering from psychological torture to me? Is this why mom didn't answer me in my dream?

Once I get to work, our secretary Mrs. Johnson tells me that Schmidt needs to see me in his office right away. She doesn't like it but today she is the bearer of bad news.

"It is a damn shame what happened to that boy."

I stop in my tracks and ask her. "Huh? What boy?"

"Samuel Benson. They found him with his wrists slit in his cell."

"No! When was this?"

"The guard reported it at 6. Who knows how long he had been dead. Why would a boy his age want to kill himself?"

"For some of these kids sad as it is I can understand why they have suicidal thoughts but you're right Mrs Johnson. In this case it doesn't make any sense."

"That's probably why Mr. Sunshine wants to see you now."

"Yeah. Detective Schmidt, good ole Mr. Sunshine."

CHAPTER 9

I always avoid Schmidt's office like the plague. The only time that I go there is when he just has to tell me some bad news about a client. It is as if he wallows in the pain that he could cause. I don't bother to knock and there he is with his feet on his desk and talking on the phone in his gray suit coat, black tie and white wrinkled shirt, talking about a man going to jail for twenty years with a big smile on his face.

"They'd all be liked up if it were up to me. They're savages." Schmidt tells the person on the other end of the line.

"You wanted to see me?" I ask.

"Yeah, yeah. I'll call you back. The new messiah is here to deliver me from evil." He looks at me smirking.

"Don't you knock? I know a nice Jewish boy like you was taught some manners."

"Mrs. Johnson said you wanted to see me? Come on Schmidt. I don't have all day."

"I can't believe what happened to Sammy. I mean he was such an upstanding citizen."

"I'm sure you're all broken up inside. I mean after

all you were so concerned about him that you went to Mrs. Bridges to ask about him. And of course you were a professional perfect gentleman. Weren't you?"

"That's the way I wrote it in my report. That old lady is the last thing on my mind."

"And the first thing?"

"You want to know something funny Blume?"

"Sure I could use a good laugh right about now."

It wasn't like Schmidt but I notice that he is slightly slurring his speech. He takes a pencil and begins tapping on top of his desk.

"Benson's cell mates told me something that was very strange. They told me that the only person that he could trust was you."

"That's impossible. Remember you introduced me to the kid."

"That's what I thought. But he told them about how much Mrs. Bridges thought that you were such an outstanding man with great integrity. Would've thought that she was talking about Jesus himself."

"Sam sure did a lot of talking before dying."

"You'd be surprised how much a man talks when he sees the grim reaper."

"Does he wear a buzz cut and a gray suit?"

"Who are you talking about Blume?"

"The grim reaper."

"I wouldn't talk like that if I were you Jew boy."

"Schmidt, I'm not an old lady that you can scare push around and scare half to death."

"Ooooh. I'm shaking now. You know what Blume? I'm keeping an eye on you. Samuel Benson made a great deal of money selling dope and the justice system won't rest until all of the loose ends are tied."

"Is that all Schmidt?"

"How are your wife and kid? Is she still cozying up to cop killers?" Of course he is talking about Raymond Rodriguez and the Mullins Case. Detective Fred Mullins was known for shaking down drug dealers for hush money. A small time dealer by the name of Raymond Rodriguez had been beaten by Mullins about two days before a horrible accident that led to Mullins' death. The police department and District Attorney were trying to have Rodriguez convicted for murder, on the basis that Mullins was killed in pursuit of Rodriguez. His Public Defender, who knew all about Mullins' operation, defended him fiercely and Rodriguez was not convicted. As fate would have it his attorney was Amber.

Looking at Schmidt, I can feel my hand slowly clenching into a fist. My heart is beating just a little faster but a sense of calm is slowly, deliberately coming over me. At that moment I jump over his desk. There I am face to face with him. He springs up in a second and I can smell the gin on his breath.

"Don't you ever ask me about my family again!"

"Like I said Blume the justice system won't rest until all of the loose ends are tied."

I turned around and walk back to my desk. Maria can see the fury in my eyes and it leaves her speechless.

CHAPTER 10

A week goes by, and then one evening after my last session with a 14 year old who was in for burglary, I am getting ready to go home. I hadn't seen Schmidt all day and it was a welcomed relief. He had stopped talking to me all together. He would walk right pass me with the menacing look of a Rottweiler ready to tear me to shreds. He was getting sloppy. He no longer bothered to iron his clothes and made it no secret that he was drinking every night. I leave my office get in my car and start to drive.

When I get home Amber and Danny are already sitting at the dinner table.

"Hi pop."

"Did you hit a homer today son?" I bend down and kiss Danny on his forehead not wanting his innocence to go away so that he doesn't have to face things like what I am going through now.

"No, but I got four hits!"

I walk over to Amber and give her a light peck on her cheek. She squeezes my hand reassuring me of the strength that we have together. The phone rings and I answer.

"Hello."

"Why hello Mr. Blume. How are you?"

"Yes a…. Mr. Van.. I'm sorry. Mr. Lerner, how are you?" I almost call him by the name that was in Danny's library book.

"I am fine. I need you to come over right away."

"But, I'm about to have dinner with my———"

"Mr. Blume. I need you to come help me with something very important."

"But"

"What is it Josh. It's our family time." Says Amber.

"Hold on a second Mr. Lerner." I cover the receiver with my hand and say to Amber, "It's Mr. Lerner he said that he needs my help."

"Well, I guess you're going to go see what he wants right?"

"It won't take long will it Mr. Lerner?"

"That's entirely up to you my friend. When you come the front door of the building will be open. Walk down the stairs to your left and come to the basement. That door will also be open. Please make sure that they are locked behind you."

"I'll be right back, Amber."

I cross the street careful not to get in the way of four girls playing hopscotch. The doors to his place are open just as Mr. Lerner said they would be. Walking down the stairs I feel the temperature becoming a bit cooler. I hear drops of water coming from a faucet, one by one and the muffled sounds of someone trying to scream.

When I make it to the basement, I stand there staring in disbelief at the sight of a Nazi soldier in full uniform. Mr. Lerner had fully transformed into; General Van Leeren. This kind and generous neighbor, who had saved my son's life, suddenly transformed into a member of one of the most ruthless killing machines ever known to humanity. He had made his confession to me the day that I returned from the hospital, but seeing him like this left me confused and terrified. There was a part of me that did not want to accept this side of his reality. And when I look to his right I suddenly realize that the muffled sounds that I had heard were coming from, Detective Schmidt.

Van Leeren has him tied to a chair and Schmidt is bleeding from the right side of his forehead. His mouth is held shut by thick duct tape. He is squirming and trying to get out of the chair.

"I believe that you know this gentleman. Don't you Mr. Blume? I was sweeping my stairs this afternoon and I noticed that this fine officer of the law had gone into your home without your permission. Can you believe that?"

"Uhhh no." Knowing Schmidt's character and current state of desperation it didn't surprise me at all. But, "no" was all that I was able to say under this extremely strange circumstance that looks and feels like a dream in which all of the characters and scenarios in your life come together.

"I believe that this belongs to you." Lerner hands me our framed picture of me with Danny and Amber.

"The good officer was holding it, with a menacing smile. I think that he was so distracted by it that he didn't even notice the blow coming from me that would put him to sleep. And now here we are."

Van Leeren holds Schmidt's gun to his head as he talks with a smile, his eyes as alert as ever.

"Mr. Blume will you please go to the refrigerator and pour us a couple of glasses of fine German Pilsner? I was saving it for a special occasion. You will find two small glasses next to the sink."

I want to stay calm so I do just as he asks. I follow his instructions, go to the refrigerator and see the beer. I can still hear the girls outside calling letters and numbers in their game of hopscotch as I slowly pour the beer into the glasses.

"Thank you Mr. Blume. You can put them down on the table there, and we will get ready for our toast."

"To what are we drinking? Things don't look so good for Detective Schmidt here."

"To the beauty of life Mr Blume, to your lovely and very beautiful wife, to your healthy son, to your mother and aunt, to my child and loving wife, all taken way too soon… to life that can drop us in the deepest and loneliest of places and yet allow us to hear the birds sing come spring. We drink to all of these precious things, but most of all we drink to redemption Mr. Blume!"

Then with one swift motion he rips the duct tape from Schmidt's sweaty face.

"Aaarh! You fuckin' crazy old man! You better get me outta here fuckin' Jew boy!"

Van Leeren then slaps Schmidt with a vicious backhand.

"How dare you speak to my guest that way? Can you believe that such ignorance still exist in the world Mr. Blume?"

"Look Mr. Lerner, I mean General Van Leeren, I appreciate you trying to help me but.. I don't think this is the way of making everything right. Let's just call the police so that they can take him away."

"Take him where for what Mr. Blume? This man who is sworn to uphold the law broke into your home. And by the way he was looking at that picture, he had every intention of doing something cruel to you or your family. Is that right or fair or just?"

"Look at this point I don't think that I know what those words mean anymore. But I know that this doesn't feel like it should be happening."

"The good Detective Schmidt has given me a chance at redemption. And once that is done, I will join my dear Hannah and Mia."

"What do you mean?" I ask the question although I knew exactly what he is thinking.

"I am going to need your help Mr. Blume. On my kitchen table, I have left documents and photos that reveal my true identity. You are going to need them when this is all over, because I know that you will not fail me."

He hands me the Luger from his holster. I was visibly shaking and sweat started running from my forehead. The sound of the dripping faucet gets louder with each drop.

"Put it down Van Leeren! This can't happen." I scream.

"Don't worry. Just think about your aunt gasping for breath on top of a pile of lifeless bodies. When you fulfill your destiny today."

"When I what?"

Then without hesitating he pulls out another gun and puts two bullets into Schmidt's head. Then he looks at me. He takes my arm steadies it and places the tip of the Luger on his forehead.

"Do it! You will be the hero who killed a war criminal, do it!"

Bang! I pull the trigger and Van Leeren falls to the ground, with a smile on his face. It is the most peaceful that I have ever seen him.

I pick up the phone and describe this crazy scene to the police. When they arrive they see Van Leeren and Schmidt dead. They take me in for questioning and believe that everything had happened just as I said it did. True to his word the documents explained in detail Mr. Lerner's past as a Nazi general. It also helped that they had seen the deterioration in Schmidt and were already suspicious of him. They already had gathered surveillance pictures of him meeting and exchanging money with kids who worked for him selling heroin to a never ending supply of fools with no hope. Amber and Danny were waiting for me at the station when they let me go.

"I love you. Are you alright?" Amber hugs me and Danny is standing there between us.

"Better than I have ever been Amber. I love you."

Printed in the United States
by Baker & Taylor Publisher Services